# TINGA LAYO

Retold by STEVEN ANDERSON

Illustrated by DAN TAYLOR

CANTATA
LEARNING

WWW.CANTATALEARNING.COM

CANTATA
LEARNING

Published by Cantata Learning
1710 Roe Crest Drive
North Mankato, MN 56003
www.cantatalearning.com

Library of Congress Control Number: 2015932796

Anderson, Steven

Tingalayo / retold by Steven Anderson; Illustrated by Dan Taylor
Series: Sing-along Animal Songs
Audience: Ages: 3–8; Grades: PreK–3
Summary: A beautiful Caribbean song about a spirited little donkey that does more than just kick up his heels. This special guy talks and even eats with a knife and fork!
1. Stories in rhyme. 2. Donkeys—fiction.

ISBN: 978-1-63290-372-3 (library binding/CD)
ISBN: 978-1-63290-503-1 (paperback/CD)
ISBN: 978-1-63290-533-8 (paperback)

Book design and art direction, Tim Palin Creative
Editorial direction, Flat Sole Studio
Music direction, Elizabeth Draper
Music arranged and produced by MusicalYouth Productions

Printed in the United States of America in North Mankato, Minnesota.
122015    0326CGS16

Tingalayo is the name of a **donkey**. People have been singing a song about him for years. Why? Because Tingalayo is **unique**. He **listens** when he is called. He talks, too! What else can this donkey do?

To find out, turn the page and sing along!

Tingalayo! Come, little donkey, come.
Tingalayo! Come, little donkey, come.

My donkey walks. My donkey talks.
My donkey eats with a knife and fork.

My donkey walks. My donkey talks.
My donkey eats with a knife and fork.

Tingalayo! Come, little donkey, come.
Tingalayo! Come, little donkey, come.

My donkey eats. My donkey sleeps.
My donkey kicks with his two **hind** feet!

My donkey eats. My donkey sleeps.
My donkey kicks with his two hind feet!

My donkey yes. My donkey no.
My donkey moves when I tell him "go!"

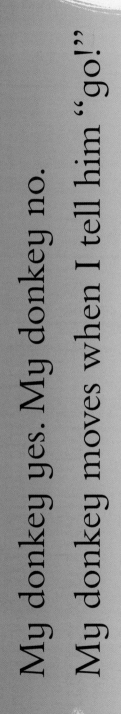

My donkey yes. My donkey no.
My donkey moves when I tell him "go!"

Tingalayo! Come, little donkey, come.
Tingalayo! Come, little donkey, come.

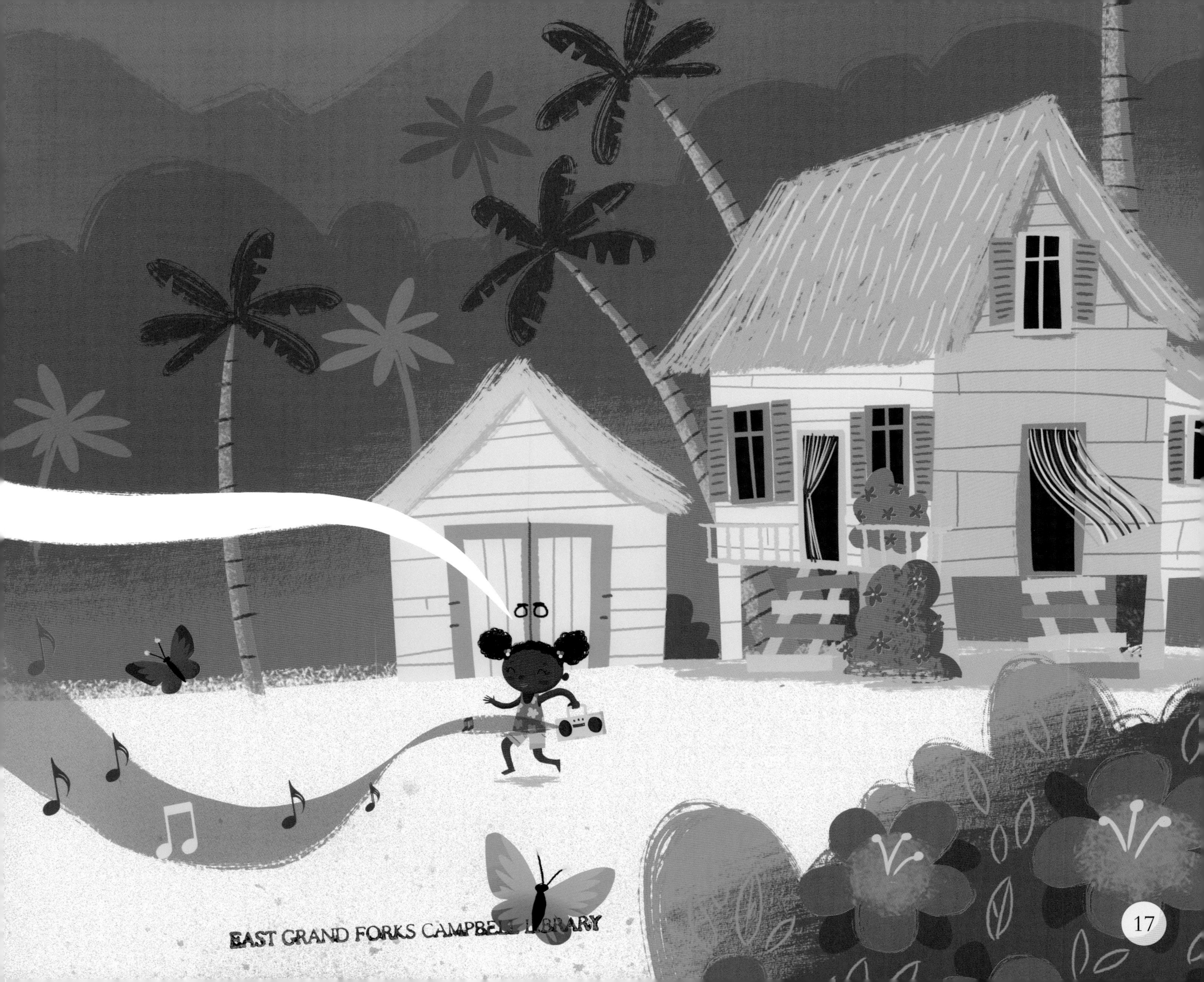

EAST GRAND FORKS CAMPBELL LIBRARY

My donkey hees. My donkey haws.
My donkey sits on the kitchen floor!